For Olaf, with love
~ G.H.

LITTLE TIGER PRESS
An imprint of Magi Publications
1 The Coda Centre, 189 Munster Road, London SW6 6AW
www.littletigerpress.com

First published in Great Britain 2002
by Little Tiger Press, London.
This edition published 2007

Text copyright © Jane Johnson 2002
Illustrations copyright © Gaby Hansen 2002

Ready for Bed!

Jane Johnson

illustrated by Gaby Hansen

LITTLE TIGER PRESS

Mrs. Rabbit sighed when all of her children were tucked safely into bed. "Ah, peace and quiet at last," she said.

But Mrs. Rabbit had spoken too soon.

"Mommy, I can't sleep," said her youngest child,
Little Bunny, interrupting her first snore.

Mrs. Rabbit tried a gentle lullaby.
  "Hush-a-bye bunny on the tree top,
    When the bough breaks, the cradle . . ."
Little Bunny's eyes began to close.
"Is my bunny sleepy now?" whispered
  Mrs. Rabbit, so as not to wake the others.

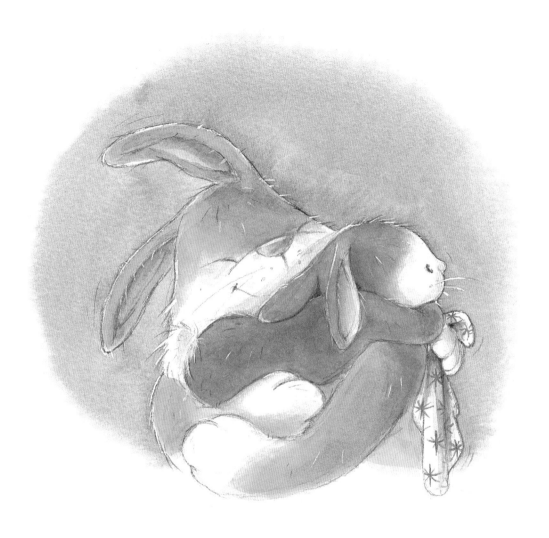

"No!" said Little Bunny. "I'm not sleepy at all." He wanted to stay up all night long with his mommy.

Mrs. Rabbit tried a bubbly bath.
"Rub-a-dub-dub, my bunny needs a scrub,"
she laughed. "Who's my Little Bunny?"
"I am!" said Little Bunny, smiling sweetly.

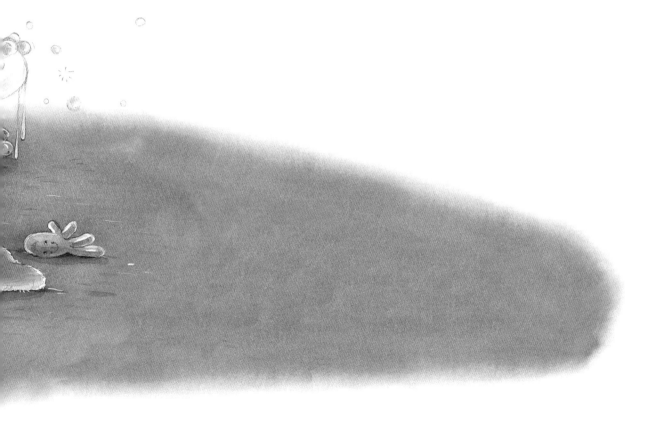

"Well now, darling, I think it's bedtime,"
Mrs. Rabbit said hopefully, drying his fur.

"No!" said Little Bunny. "It's not bedtime yet."

Mrs. Rabbit tried warm milk. "Swirly, whirly, creamy white," she yawned. "Time to cuddle and say 'Good night.'"

"Cuddle, yes! 'Good night,' no!" said
Little Bunny. He wanted to stay up with
his mommy forever.

"Squeezy, huggy, snuggle up tight," he said happily.
"Am I the best little bunny
  in the world tonight?"

"I love all my bunnies the same, sleepyhead," said Mrs. Rabbit.

"Then I'll never be ready for bed,"
said Little Bunny.

"What am I going to do with you?"
said his worn-out mother. Little Bunny
jumped up excitedly . . .

"Let's play bunny hops!"
said Little Bunny.

"Hoppity, hoppity, hop . . .

'round and 'round the
room till I . . ."

"Flop!" whispered
Mrs. Rabbit.

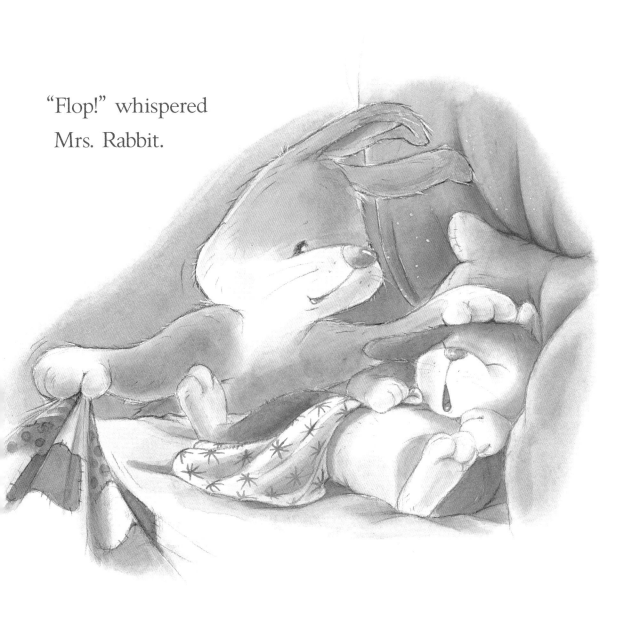

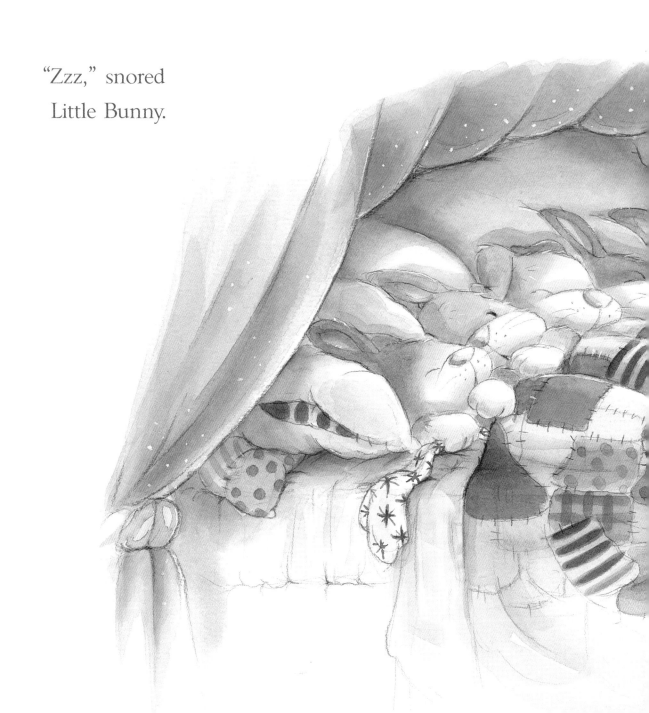

"Zzz," snored
Little Bunny.

"Ah, peace and quiet at last,"
sighed Mrs. Rabbit. "Even my
youngest bunny is asleep in bed."

Mrs. Rabbit flopped into
bed, but through her
snores she heard . . .

her second youngest bunny call out,
"Mommy, I can't sleep!"